To beautiful Sandy Island,

and to the memory of its director, Nathan Todaro—J.S.

For Scott and Stephanie Miscione—T.L.

Library of Congress Cataloging-in-Publication Data
Slepian, Jan. Lost moose / Jan Slepian; illustrated by Ted Lewin.   p.   cm.
Summary: A moose calf separated from his mother encounters a boy who follows him on a
long walk through the woods, until they are both reclaimed by their respective mothers.
1. Moose—Juvenile fiction. [1. Moose—Fiction.] I. Lewin, Ted, ill. II. Title.
PZ10.3.S427Lo 1995   [E]—dc20   94-6738 CIP AC   ISBN 0-399-22749-0
10 9 8 7 6 5 4 3 2 1
First Impression

Jan Slepian

Lost Moose

illustrated by Ted Lewin

Philomel Books
New York

The moose and her calf had ranged far from their small home island together, searching for young plants and roots. Then one summer night she led him into the water to swim to another island.

When they were in the middle of the lake, a storm arose without warning. The wind whipped up the waves and sent the rain slantwise. The moose and her little one became separated in the wild water.

The young moose reached the island without his mother. Trees sheltered him from the wind. He was tired from the dangerous swim. For the first time he slept without his mother nearby.

The next morning the storm was over. The moose woke to an island thick with woods at one end and people at the other. On this vacation island, families slept in cabins and ate together in a big dining hall.

Luckily, he had landed at the wooded part, where there were no people.

He came to a small pond. Plants covered the water like a green carpet. A family of ducks was paddling through the plants. The young moose waded through the shallow water, tearing at his green breakfast. Plant stems hung from his mouth like straws.

He was hungry. There were plenty of fresh leaves and new twigs to eat. There were exciting new smells to explore, and no mother to stop him when he followed his nose. He lifted his head and sent a high, free sound from his throat.

Not far from the duck pond was James's cabin. Every morning before breakfast he came to feed the ducks. He carried bread saved from supper the night before in the dining hall. His mother always wrapped it for him in a paper napkin.

That morning, when James saw the strange animal in the duck pond, he froze with one foot in the air and breathed in hard. He knew to be quiet.

What could it be? He looked hard at its long nose, and then in a flash he knew. It was one of Santa Claus's reindeer. Hadn't he seen pictures of them in books? Only no antlers, he noted carefully.

James thought to himself, Okay, this one must be a beginner. It's just learning to be a Christmas reindeer. Still it must belong to Santa Claus and somehow wandered away from him all the way here. That was no surprise to James, since he liked to wander too. His mother was always looking for him.

James said to himself, "It's lost, and I found it first."

His heart bumped in his chest. Maybe Santa would come for his lost reindeer. When that happened James would be right there. He would walk right up and say hi. Santa Claus would not forget him.

Suddenly the young moose saw James and stopped feeding. He stepped sideways on his long, thin legs. His nose tested the air. Was that a danger smell? His mother wasn't there to tell him.

The moose stepped out of the pond and moved into the woods. James followed him.

Underfoot the pine needles were as thick as a mattress. Overhead the branches met to hide the sky. It was shady and quiet in the forest. The moose moved along slowly. Whenever it stopped to nibble a twig, James stopped too. Soundlessly, in the same easy way, the moose and the boy slipped through the woods together as if joined by a cord.

The sound of a bell broke the silence. James looked quickly to the treetops. Maybe it was Santa's sled.

The top branches didn't stir. A worry walked into James's head. It was summertime, daytime. Santa wouldn't want to be seen. How would he come for his reindeer?

The little moose had stopped at the strange noise. He stood on a mound of moss, alert and still.

James sent a message to him silently: "Don't worry. I won't let anything hurt you."

As if the animal had heard, he bent his head and continued his walk under the sheltering trees.

Again James heard the bell. *Clang clang.* Now he knew it was the breakfast bell calling everyone to the dining hall. His mother would be looking for him.

But the thoughts of his mother and breakfast went right out of James's head. He followed the moose through the shadowy woods and didn't think of anything else.

The gloom of the forest began to lift. Sunlight sprinkled the floor. There were fewer trees.

The moose stepped out of the woods under an open sky. Then James knew where they were. It was the worst possible place for them to be.

Down the path was the dining hall, full of noise, full of people.

The boy jumped in front of the animal and waved his arms. "Go back!" he shouted. "Go back!"

At that moment there was a rushing through the trees like the rising of a rough wind. At this sound the little moose tossed his head. His nose searched the air.

James heard it too and backed away. Something was happening. Santa was coming. James would know him even if he became the wind itself.

But it was the mother moose!

She had found the island at last and had come for her calf. She draped her neck about him.

James's mother also had been searching everywhere for her child. She came up the path and saw him near the large animal, then ran to snatch him.

The mother moose pushed her calf behind her. James's mother pushed James behind her.

The two mothers stared at one another.

In a swift movement it was over. The moose and her calf withdrew into the woods. The little moose turned his head once to look back at James. Then he followed his mother to the water and safely back to his home island.

James followed his mother. He was close to tears. She had told him that what they had seen was a mother moose and her calf. He had said to her quickly, "I know that!" Disappointment made his nose stuffy.

As they walked down the path to the dining hall, James smelled the piney woods. He saw again the young reindeer looking back at him and began to smile.

There had been magic in the walk that morning after all.